The Runaway Garden

A delicious story that's good for you,too!

BY JEFFERY L. SCHATZER

ILLUSTRATIONS BY JEFFREY EBBELER

mitten press

All inquiries should be addressed to:

Mitten Press

An imprint of Ann Arbor Media Group LLC

2500 S. State Street

Ann Arbor, MI 48104

Printed and bound in China.

10   9   8   7   6   5   4   3   2

Library of Congress Cataloging-in-Publication Data

Schatzer, Jeffery L.
The runaway garden : a delicious story that's good for you, too!
by Jeffery L. Schatzer ; illustrated by Jeffrey Ebbeler.
p. cm.
Summary: When a young girl gets tired of working in the garden and threatens to run away,
her grandfather tells her a story about the night the vegetables left the garden.
ISBN-13: 978-1-58726-436-8 (hardcover : alk. paper)
ISBN-10: 1-58726-436-6
[1. Vegetables--Fiction. 2. Gardening--Fiction. 3. Conduct of life--Fiction. 4. Grandfathers--Fiction.
5. Stories in rhyme.] I. Ebbeler, Jeffrey, ill. II. Title.
PZ8.3.S29712Run 2007
[E]--dc22

2006035737Book design by Somberg Design
www.sombergdesign.com

"I really, really hate this job!" I yelled and threw a fit.
"The work's too hard! My fingers hurt! I don't like this one bit!
If Grandpa makes me pull more weeds, there is no way I'll stay.
I'll pack a bag of dolls and things and leave this very day!"

Still mad that night, I took a seat on our squeaky back porch swing.

Grandpa sat beside me, but I wouldn't say a thing.

He handed me a toothpick, as he put one in his mouth.

The stars came out as the moon hung low, cradled softly in the south.

"It was a clear and starry night like this," Grandpa began to say.
"That the vegetables in these here parts got up and ran away.
The magic in the moonbeams or the first crisp air of fall
cast a spell on all the plants inside the garden wall."

"When their leaves grew out like arms and roots turned into feet,
they popped up from their earthen beds and headed for the street."
"I'm leaving here without delay," said rhubarb to string bean.
"I want to do what I've never done and see what I've never seen."

"Heed my words," came a raspy voice from along the dark rock wall.
The squash stepped forward, raised a vine, and tried to warn them all.
"We know not of the outside world, the garden is our home.
It's not safe for garden plants to wander or to roam."

"Don't listen," said the ear of corn. "I've heard it all before.
I'm tired of the garden life and know there must be more."
"That's right," said the asparagus. "I want some fun myself,
before I'm piled up with my friends upon the grocer's shelf."

"Those silly plants ignored the squash and trusted in their fate.
The potatoes all just closed their eyes and took off out the gate.
All the green peas split for town; the tomatoes stewed and stirred.
Celery and her friend sweet corn stalked off without a word."

"The radishes took off in a bunch with the turnips and the beets.
Leaf lettuce started to the west and cabbage headed east.
The peppers were the last to leave and hopped the garden wall
without a thought of 'goodbye, squash,' without a thought at all."

"It was quite a sight to see," I heard ol' Grandpa say.
"The night they magically grew their legs and up and ran away.
Throughout the countryside that night the plants ran far and wide.
They played games and sang their songs. Some even chose to hide."

"At first the veggies thought it great to scamper around so free.
But it wasn't long before things went wrong, that is, if you ask me.
Even the berries got in a jam before the night was done.
I guess those silly plants found out that running away's no fun."

Grandpa swirled the toothpick in his mouth … "I wish I had a nickel
for every cucumber and beet that got into a pickle.
Some pumpkins got themselves squashed flat, and radishes all turned red.
Peppers popped, snap beans snapped, and a cauliflower lost its head."

"Before the yawning rays of dawn, they made their way back home.
Each said 'I'm sorry' to the squash, vowing never again to roam."
Then Grandpa winked. He squeezed me close and whispered in my ear,
"What can we learn from the vegetables? What can we learn, my dear?"

I spun the toothpick in my mouth, just like my Grandpa did,
took his large, worn hand in mine, and this is what I said,
"We've all got a place to be and special jobs to do, you see.
That includes the vegetables, but also you and me."

We snuggled late into the night on that creaky wooden swing.
The time passed quickly as we swung, though we didn't say a thing.
Just before I fell asleep in the moon's soft golden wash,
I kissed my Grandpa's baldy head.
From then on, I called him "Squash."